To all the kids who love Pete the Cat!
Stay groovy!
Mark 9:23
—J.D. & K.D.

Pete the Cat and the Bedtime Blues

Text copyright © 2015 by Kimberly and James Dean

Illustrations copyright © 2015 by James Dean

Pete the Cat is a registered trademark of Pete the Cat, LLC.

For information address HarperCollins Children's Books, a division of HarperCollins Publishers,

195 Broadway, New York, NY 10007.

www.harpercollinschildrens.com

Library of Congress Control Number: 2014047807

ISBN 978-0-06-230432-2

The artist used pen and ink with watercolor and acrylic paint on

300lb press paper to create the illustrations for this book.

Typography by Jeanne L. Hogle

22 23 24 25 26   PC   10 9 8 7 6 5 4 3 2 1

❖

First paperback edition, 2023

Pete the Cat
and the Bedtime Blues

Kimberly and James Dean

HARPER
An Imprint of HarperCollinsPublishers

Pete and the gang had a great day!
They'd been at the beach. Surf and
sun and tons of fun.

But when the sun went down, they didn't want the fun to end. Pete had an idea.

The party was far-out!
But they knew they couldn't stay up all night.

The gang decided it was time
to say good night.

On went the pajamas and out went the light.

Good night, Gus,
good night, Alligator,
good night, Toad,

GOOD NIGHT,

Pete was just about to catch some ZZZs when . . .

CLAP! CLAP! CLAP!

"Who did that?" Pete asked.

Pete tried again to catch some ZZZs when . . .

RAT-A-TAT-TAT!

"Who did **that?**" Pete asked.

Good night, Gus,
good night, Alligator,
good night, Toad,

GOOD NIGHT,

Pete closed his eyes to
catch some ZZZs when
he heard . . .

HOT
PIZZA

Pete had a hunch.
It was Alligator. He was always
up for eating.

What could Pete do?

All the
CLAPPING,
Rat-A-Tat-Tatting,
and
MUNCHING
was giving him the
bedtime blues.

Pete had a groovy idea.

He got out his favorite bedtime story and started to read—first to himself and then to the gang.

Pete noticed it was finally quiet.

They all settled down.
No one made a sound.

Pete yawned and turned off the light.

"Good night, sleep tight."

Time to catch some ZZZs.

Tomorrow was another day for surfing, sun, and tons of fun.